HORSE DIARIES
· Luna ·

HORSE DIARIES

HORSE DIARIES

Luna

CATHERINE HAPKA

illustrated by RUTH SANDERSON

RANDOM HOUSE NEW YORK

Text copyright © 2015 by Catherine Hapka
Cover art and interior illustrations copyright © 2015 by Ruth Sanderson
Photograph on p. 141 © Bob Langrish

All rights reserved. Published in the United States by Random House Children's Books, a division of Penguin Random House LLC, New York.

Random House and the colophon are registered trademarks of Penguin Random House LLC.

Visit us on the Web! randomhousekids.com

Educators and librarians, for a variety of teaching tools, visit us at RHTeachersLibrarians.com

Library of Congress Cataloging-in-Publication Data
Hapka, Catherine.
Luna / Catherine Hapka ; illustrated by Ruth Sanderson. — 1st ed.
p. cm. — (Horse diaries ; 12)
Summary: In the Netherlands in 1855, May, a young member of a circus family who is not permitted to perform because of a twisted foot, bonds with a local Friesian farm horse that she names Luna, and together the two perform a heroic act that changes their futures for the better. Includes facts about Friesian horses.
ISBN 978-0-553-53370-5 (trade) — ISBN 978-0-553-53371-2 (lib. bdg.) — ISBN 978-0-553-53372-9 (ebook)
1. Friesian horse—Juvenile fiction. 2. Netherlands—History—19th century—Juvenile fiction. [1. Friesian horse—Fiction. 2. Horses—Fiction. 3. Circus—Fiction. 4. Netherlands—History—19th century—Fiction.] I. Sanderson, Ruth, illustrator. II. Title.
PZ10.3.H2258Lun 2015 [Fic]—dc23 2015000450

Printed in the United States of America
10 9 8 7 6 5 4 3 2 1
First Edition

This book has been officially leveled by using the F&P Text Level Gradient™ Leveling System.

In memory of Jennifer Reed and all of her horses

—C.H.

Thanks to all my character models:
Elizabeth, Abby, Lew, Eric, Jennifer, Joey, and Jeff.
And a special thanks to Sophia and her lovely
Friesian mare, Froukje.

—R.S.

CONTENTS

"Oh! if people knew what a comfort to horses a light hand is . . ."

—from *Black Beauty*, by Anna Sewell

HORSE DIARIES
· Luna ·

Friesland, the Netherlands, Summer, 1855

Until my fifth summer, I knew nothing of the world beyond the quiet country village where I was foaled. I lived my first year in a beautiful green pasture with my dam and several other horses. After weaning, I spent another year or more with a herd of young fillies, eating and playing and napping in the sun. Soon the humans taught me to pull a carriage, which I found easy and pleasant work.

Then one morning, a young man from my farm led me along a dusty lane past windmills and fields of grazing cows and sheep. Finally we arrived at a different farm on the far side of the village. There I met my new owner, a kind man with white hair and a wrinkled face who was known as Gerrit. He brought me into his small wooden barn, where I met his other horse, a tall gelding named Coal, along with various sheep, dogs, and poultry.

I felt unsettled at first, being away from everything I'd known. But I remained as calm as I could and soon discovered that life here was agreeable enough. Little was asked of me aside from pulling Gerrit's carriage to town now and then.

The stall where I stayed at night was roomy and comfortable, and the grass in the pasture sweet and plentiful. Gerrit and his hired man, a husky youth from the village named Kai, were kind and patient with all the animals.

Soon after my arrival, I asked Coal why our owner's eyes always looked so sad. Coal nodded and considered my question, slow and deliberate as he always was to think and respond. *We horses prefer to live in herds*, he said.

Yes, I agreed. I missed my old companions. It was much quieter here, with only one other horse and the small flock of sheep for company.

Humans are similar, Coal went on. *Except they often prefer to live in pairs, like geese.*

I knew little of geese, except that they were noisy and brash. Luckily Coal wasn't finished.

When I came here, he went on, *Gerrit did not live alone on this farm, and he rarely looked sad. His wife lived here with him. She used to bring me apples nearly every day.*

My stomach rumbled at the mention of apples. At my old farm, the children had sometimes brought us those tasty treats from the orchard near the house.

Where is this wife now? I asked, wondering if she might bring us apples.

Coal shook his head slowly, causing his thick mane to swing. *She is no longer here,* he said. *She died last cold season, or so said the dogs.*

Gerrit's two dogs were busy creatures, always full of news from their explorations throughout the countryside. This news often involved dead creatures, from hares to birds to snakes—though rarely humans.

Coal regarded me with his large, dark eyes. *Now Gerrit lives here alone with his animals,* he said. *That is why he is sad.*

Two years passed. By then, Gerrit and Coal were as familiar to me as my dam and other companions had once been. My life was quiet and easy.

Then one day things changed again. Oh, not at first—that morning, Gerrit came into the barn as he did every day, with the dogs at his heel. Though his eyes were as sad as ever, he was whistling, and his step was livelier than usual.

"Good morning, Dark Girl," Gerrit said, giving me a pat as he passed my stall. "And hello to you, too, Coal."

Kai hurried into the barn. "Should we keep the sheep and horses in the farmyard, Gerrit?" the hired man asked, nudging the smaller dog out of his way as he headed for the sheep pen. "They might spook at the circus folk setting up their tent in the meadow."

Gerrit chuckled. "Perhaps the silly sheep will," he said. "But not my two good stout horses! Isn't that right, you two?"

I had no idea what he meant, but that wasn't unusual. Humans were full of words, so many that it was impossible for a horse to keep track.

"Let's take the horses first, then," Kai said. "Come on, Coal, old fella."

As Kai led Coal out of his stall, Gerrit came for me. I walked with him through the barn and outside. I saw nothing unusual in the small farmyard, but when Coal reached the gate, he stopped suddenly and seemed to grow taller as he raised his head to stare at something across the pasture.

What is it? I asked him.

Something new, he responded with a snort. *Something different.*

After a few more steps, I saw it, too. On the far side of our pasture lay a large fallow field. Normally it was vacant, aside from birds and other wild creatures.

But not today. "Relax, fella," Kai said with a pat for Coal. "It's just the circus."

I stretched my neck upward to see better, not wishing to move forward until I was certain it was safe to do so. At least a dozen humans were bustling about in the middle of the field, though they weren't my concern—humans caused me no fear. There were four or five pale-colored horses tied up and grazing, along with several dogs running around barking and doing what dogs did. None of that was cause for alarm, either.

However, I could also see a large bundle of brightly colored fabric, which rippled with every touch of wind in a most disquieting way. I watched with caution as the humans shouted and then raised part of this fabric, causing it to stand up as tall as the barn roof. The breeze caught it again, turning it into something resembling a live creature that bucked and swayed in the air. Could there be creatures lurking inside causing it to move that way, or was it truly only the wind? It was difficult to tell for sure. The dogs barked and leaped about nearby, seemingly excited by the activity. Were they worried about the fabric monster, too?

Coal was keeping one eye on the odd fabric and the dogs, but he was also sniffing the light breeze blowing toward us. *Do you smell that?* he said. *What can it be?*

I knew the scent he meant. I had smelled it, too, mingling with the scents of humans and dogs and horses. It was clearly an animal, but unlike any animal I'd ever smelled before. It smelled wild and raw and frightening in a way I couldn't describe.

I don't know what it is, I said, still watching the fabric carefully. *Do you think it's dangerous?*

The men had been standing with us, allowing us time to take in the strange sights. Now Gerrit gave a tug on my halter. "Come along, Dark Girl," he said. "You'll be okay."

His voice was as calm and confident as ever. I lowered my head, reassured by his attitude. Surely if there was something dangerous out there, a deadly monster hiding in the fabric, Gerrit would not ask me to move toward it. He had always treated me well, and that made me trust him.

Coal reached the same conclusion, and soon we were stepping into our pasture. As soon as the men released us, we walked closer to the far fence line for a better look at the activity beyond.

What are they doing? Coal wondered.

The humans were still moving around the fabric hump. It was starting to take the shape of a

building, like a barn but much larger. We watched as the humans raised another section, shouting to each other as they worked.

A few minutes later, Gerrit and Kai herded the sheep into the pasture with help from the dogs. The sheep didn't notice the commotion in the meadow at first. But when one of them did catch sight of the swaying fabric building, she let out a bleat of alarm and leaped about trying to hide behind her companions. This alerted the other sheep, and they all ran around in a tizzy for a while until their hunger overwhelmed their fear.

Meanwhile, Coal and I grazed near the fence, watching the activity in the meadow between bites. That strange scent still hung on the breeze, mixing with more familiar smells of dogs and human food and other things, but before long I stopped noticing it as much. I spent some time watching the horses, marveling at their pale coats, which gleamed in the sunlight. Most of the horses I'd known had coats as dark as the night sky, with thick manes and flowing feathers of hair covering their lower legs. But these horses' manes and tails were silky and thin, and they had no feathers.

Perhaps their owners clipped off the feathers, Coal guessed when I mentioned it.

Why would they do that? I stared at a delicate-looking dappled mare with an arched neck as she nipped at a gelding who was crowding her.

Why do humans do anything they do? Coal replied. *It's better not to wonder too much, Dark Girl.*

I supposed he was right. But I couldn't help wondering all the same. Occasionally the pale horses would look our way, but they never came

closer, and I guessed that they were tied or hobbled in place.

By the time Gerrit and Kai reappeared to
lead us back to the barn at the end of the day,
I'd nearly lost interest in the pale horses and the
rest of the circus. The fabric building seemed to
be complete. It had taken on a rounded shape,
with flags that flapped in the wind and occasionally startled the sheep, though Coal and I paid
them no mind. That strange scent was still there,
but we couldn't smell it once we were inside our
barn and soon forgot to wonder about it, focusing instead on our grain and hay. Gerrit and Kai
chatted about the circus as they performed their
evening chores, although I hardly listened.

Soon the men left and the barn was quiet
except for the cooing of hens, the occasional

bleat of a sheep, and Coal's steady chewing as he ate his hay. Sometime after that, I was dozing off when I heard the door creak open.

I lifted my head, expecting to see Gerrit coming in to check on one of the pregnant ewes, as he sometimes did. But it wasn't my master's familiar figure who stepped in.

"Hello," a girl's soft voice called into the dim barn. "Anyone in here?"

2

Meeting May

I let out a curious snort as the girl entered the
barn. She heard me and turned toward my stall.
Now I could see that she was perhaps half grown,
with dark hair and lively brown eyes in a pale face.

"Oh, hello," she said, reaching up to pat my
nose. "Aren't you a pretty horse!"

I lowered my head so she could reach, sniffing at her as she stroked my face and neck. Her scent was pleasant and clean, though I caught a faint whiff of that mystery smell clinging to her clothes. She moved on to pat Coal and the sheep as well, and even cooed over the sleepy hens on their roosts. But then she returned to me.

I was glad. I'd been watching her as she explored the barn, liking the smell and sound of her and her gentle energy. There was something unusual about her movement that caught my eye, though she was so quick and unpredictable that I couldn't figure out what had attracted my attention. She smiled at me as I lowered my head to her again.

"What's your name, pretty girl?" she murmured as she ran her slim fingers through my forelock. I felt her fingers probing my forehead. She parted my forelock and peered up at my face. "Oh, look at this—you're not black all over like I thought! See?" she said. "You have a little white marking right here. It looks like a crescent moon." A smile broke across her face. "I knew you were special! You're not just like all the other big black horses around these parts. You're unique! I think you need a special name—how about Luna? Do you like that, girl? Hmm?"

I didn't understand all of what she said. But the word *Luna* lingered in my ear like the music of Gerrit's humming, and I nodded with pleasure at the sound of it.

That made the girl laugh. "You *do* like it!" she exclaimed. "Well, good. Then it's nice to meet you, Luna. My name is May. My family just arrived here with our traveling circus."

Coal was watching from his stall. He let out a snort. *What is the young human doing here?* he asked me.

I don't know, I said. *But I like her.*

Hmm. After watching for a moment more, the other horse returned his attention to his hay.

May rubbed my nose, still chattering cheerfully. "I love traveling around everywhere," she said, her fingers working their way over the itchy spots on my poll and behind my ears. "It's fun to explore different cities and villages and see new things. I especially like seeing all the different animals in the different towns and countries. Of course, the horses are always my favorite!"

She took her hands away, and for a moment I was disappointed. Then I saw that she was fiddling with the latch on my stall door. Soon she swung it open, and I was able to lower my head farther toward her. When I did so, she laughed with delight and hugged my head, which was nearly as long as her entire torso.

"Oh, Luna, I'm glad I chose this direction to explore!" she exclaimed. "You're sweet! But here—hasn't anyone combed out your mane lately?"

She went to work with her fingers. Like all horses of my type, I had a thick, long mane hanging nearly to my shoulders. Gerrit or Kai occasionally ran a comb through it, but they weren't nearly as gentle as May's careful fingers as she teased out each knot and tangle.

And still she talked, telling me how beautiful I was and promising to visit every night while the circus was in town. "My family doesn't know I sneak away at night," she confided, leaning closer to whisper into my ear. "But I know you won't tell them, Luna." She giggled. Then she fell silent, and when she finally spoke again, her voice was sad. "It doesn't matter, anyway. It's not as if I'm needed much during the day, so nobody even notices if I sleep a little later than everyone else." She sighed and was quiet for another long moment. I turned my head—careful not to bump into her—and nudged at her shoulder, wishing she didn't look so sad.

That made her laugh again. She hugged me, pressing her small head against my larger one.

"Oh, Luna," she said. "Never mind all that. I'd better get back before I'm missed. But I'll visit you again—I promise!"

Over the next several nights, May returned to see me. I looked forward to her arrival, listening for the sound of her footsteps and the sight of her small figure slipping through the barn door.

On her second visit, May brought a comb. She used it to work out the last of the tangles in my mane and tail. When that was finished, she went to work on the long black feathers on my legs, combing out the burrs and chunks of mud until the hair lay smooth and silky over my hooves.

The morning after that visit, Gerrit glanced down as he led me out of my stall. His eyebrows rose, and he pursed his lips and let out a soft hmmph.

"What is it, Gerrit?" Kai asked, glancing over from outside Coal's stall.

"Nothing, lad." Gerrit winked at me and smiled. "Let's get these beasts outside."

That night, May arrived a little later than usual. "We had our first show tonight, Luna," she told me. "Father and Mother and the others were pleased with how many people came." Her eyes took on a faraway look. "And my sister Minerva had a new costume—she looked so beautiful standing on the back of the horses as they cantered around the ring. . . ."

She continued to chatter as she quickly combed my mane and feathers. Then she stepped out of my stall and looked around the barn.

"I have an idea," she whispered. She grabbed my halter from the hook near the door. I lowered my head toward it, as I always did for the men. May slipped it on, then attached a lead rope. "Come on, girl," she said. "Let's go for a walk."

I was surprised—Gerrit rarely took me from my stall after dark unless it was to pull him to town for some late errand or social call. But I stepped out obediently after May as I'd been taught to do since I was a foal.

She led me to the door and out into the moon-lit farmyard. There she paused, grabbing a stout wooden staff leaning against the door frame. As we started across the yard, she held the staff in her free hand, using it to balance herself. Now I realized why her movement had caught my eye the first night. Out here in the open, without walls or stall doors to hold on to, she walked with a limp. It reminded me of one of the dogs on my birth farm, who'd been stepped on by a naughty colt and could never move the same way afterward.

"You'll have to walk slowly, Luna," May told me. "You see, I was born with a twisted foot, and that's why I need this cane." She sighed. "It's also why my family won't let me perform in the circus," she added, her voice sad now. "They keep me out of the spotlight and instead have me take tickets and do other boring things like that, while my sister and brothers get to perform." She clenched her fist so tightly on the lead rope that I felt her tension streaming through the soft cotton. "I know I could be a trick rider like Minerva if only they'd let me try! But they won't—they won't even let me ride anymore, ever since Uncle Claude caught me riding on my own last year."

Sensing her distress, I came to a halt and snuffled at her shoulder. She turned toward me, and in the moonlight I saw tears glistening in her eyes.

"Oh, Luna," she said. "Will things ever change for me? Will they ever let me do something useful instead of being forced to sit in the background and watch? I don't think I can stand it much longer if they don't. In fact . . ."

She hesitated, looking this way and that as if expecting to be interrupted. But the farmyard was quiet, with only a tawny owl perched on a branch nearby to witness our walk. May took a deep breath, leaning closer.

"If things don't change, I'm going to run

away," she whispered. "I'll slip out at night, just as I've been doing, and disappear in some foreign town or city where they can never find me."

I didn't really understand what she was saying. But I could tell that whatever it was, it caused her great distress. So I snuffled at her again, wishing there was a way to make her feel better. She smiled and flung her arms around me.

"Oh, Luna," she murmured. "I'm so glad I met you."

The next couple of nights went much the same. May took me for walks around the farm, telling me about her plans for the future. On the third night, she didn't talk as much and seemed distracted, staring into the night sky as I grazed. Later, she leaned on the door after returning me to my stall.

"We pack up and leave after tomorrow night's show, Luna," she blurted out. "And I've made a decision."

Sensing a new kind of mood in her, I lifted my head from my hay, which I'd started to nibble. May was staring at me with fire in her eyes.

"Things will never change unless I change them," she told me. "And I don't want to leave you. That's why I've decided to run away now—and stay here with you."

May's Plan

The following night, May arrived at the usual time. She was carrying a worn rucksack stuffed full of human items, which she hid behind the hay. I waited for her to put on my halter for our usual walk, but instead she wandered around the barn, peering at everything with sharp eyes.

"I need to find a hiding place," she said. "My family will be packing up at dawn. If they come looking for me . . ." She paused for a long moment, then shrugged. "They'll probably look around a little if they notice I'm gone," she continued. "In any case, I don't want them to find me."

What is she doing? Coal wondered as we watched May climb up to the loft, then return and poke around behind the hens' roost.

I don't know, I replied. *But she is as riled up as a dog with a fresh bone.*

Finally May came into my stall. "I suppose this is as good a place as any," she said. "They'll never expect me to be in a stall with a horse in it. At least I hope not." She rubbed my nose. "And I'll feel better being close to you, Luna."

I pricked my ears at my name, which I'd come

to recognize by then. May turned away to rustle about in my hay pile, moving it out of the front corner to a spot closer to the door. Then she crouched down where the hay had been, pulling some of my straw bedding over herself.

"There," she said, settling into the corner. "They'll never spot me here. All I have to do is stay hidden until they give up and leave without me. Once the circus has been gone awhile, I'll ask your owner for a job." She leaned her head against the rough wooden wall, gazing up at me. "I'm good with animals—I could help with the sheep and chickens. And of course I'd love taking care of you, Luna. That wouldn't seem like work at all."

I lowered my head to pick at the hay. May reached over, stroking my cheek.

"Still, I'll miss my family and the circus, at least a little." Her voice sounded wistful. "Especially Minerva, and of course my little brothers, Hugo and Oliver. Even as young as they are, they're already part of the clown troupe. They love it." She smiled. "You should see them tumbling around as if their bodies were made of rubber. . . ."

There was more, but I heard little of it as I ate my hay and then dozed for a while. The sound of May's voice was soothing, like Gerrit's humming or the morning songs of the wild birds in the meadow.

I didn't know how much time had passed when I suddenly came awake, alerted by a snort from Coal. He was staring at the barn door.

What is it? I asked.

Something outside, he said. *Humans—strangers.*

Now I heard them, too. A pair of voices outside, both male, clearly trying to whisper but too excited to stay quiet.

A moment later two youths burst into the barn. They were holding candles and large, empty sacks. Their clothes were dark and their eyes rather wild as they glanced around the place.

"Here we are, mate," one youth said. "Let's not waste any time, all right? We don't want the old man to wake up and hear us."

"Right," his friend replied. "Grab anything of value, and be quick about it."

May awoke with a start. "My family!" she whispered, cringing back into the straw. But when the youths spoke again, she frowned. "No—that's nobody I know," she murmured before falling silent, her eyes wide and frightened.

The youths didn't hear her. They were grabbing whatever they could—tools, leather goods, and more—and stuffing it all into their sacks. The sheep and hens were awake by now, too. The hens stirred uneasily on their roost.

One of the youths glanced that way. "Chickens," he said, licking his lips. "Should I grab a few? They'd make a tasty dinner."

"No, leave them," his friend said. "They'll make too much noise." He stopped in front of my stall. "Besides, if we were to risk taking any of the animals, it should be these handsome horses. Imagine how much they'd fetch at the sale in the city! And nobody would have any trouble believing that circus folk would steal good-looking horses like these for their show." He snickered and tried to pat me, but I pulled back so he couldn't quite reach.

"Don't be daft," the other youth said. "How would we sneak out of here with two enormous horses? Or even one of them, for that matter?"

His friend nodded and turned away. "You're right," he said. "We'll stick to the plan. Take anything easy to grab and sell. That'll be enough to pay our way out of this rotten town. And the best part? Nobody will ever think to blame us with those shifty circus folk about."

Both of them sniggered as they continued snatching things. I looked at May, whose eyes were wider than ever now. I wished I could comfort her, but I was feeling terribly frightened myself. Even though I couldn't understand everything these rough youths were saying, I sensed that they were up to no good. What would they do next?

We soon found out. After they'd stuffed all they could in their bags, the pair stepped to the door.

"All right," one of them said, lifting his candle.

"Let's cover our tracks and then get out of here before someone notices the fire."

He touched his candle to a straw bale near the door. It flared immediately, crackling into flame. May gasped at my feet, though the youths didn't hear. They were busy lighting a few more bales afire. Then they rushed out of the barn.

4

Fire!

As soon as the youths had disappeared, May leaped to her feet. "Oh no!" she cried. "I can't believe those scoundrels. We can't let my family take the blame! But first we have to get you all to safety."

She swung open my stall door and grabbed

my halter—one of the few things the youths hadn't stolen. This time, however, I didn't lower my head obediently to allow her to put it on me. I was watching the flames licking their way across the far wall, transfixed by the sound, the smell, the smoke. . . .

"Luna!" May said sharply. "Please—I can't reach."

The desperate tone of her voice broke through my fear. I looked down at her, and she grabbed my nose and pulled it closer, slipping the halter on quickly. Then she left me, rushing to Coal's stall.

The gelding was dancing in his doorway, snorting at the flames coming closer across the wooden floor. Even through my fear, I was concerned for my favorite girl. *Coal!* I called. *Watch out for May—don't step on her.*

Coal didn't respond for a moment. Nearby, the sheep were bleating and milling around in their pen, and all the hens were awake and shuffling about. The rooster let out a loud, strangled crow, and then another. From the direction of the house, I heard the faint sound of the dogs beginning to bark.

"Easy, big boy," May said, her voice shaking as she reached Coal's stall. "Oh no—I think they stole your halter!" She stood there for a moment, staring around uncertainly.

I kept one eye on a tongue of flame licking its way across the floor, feeding upon stray bits of hay and grain. Letting out a snort, I kicked my stall door.

That made May jump. She spun around and

grabbed the latch of Coal's door with trembling fingers, sliding it open.

"Come on out, boy," she urged. "Get away as fast as you can!"

She raced to the barn door and swung that wide open, crying out as a spark landed on her arm. Next she came to me, opening my door and reaching for me.

By now the smoke and heat filled my nostrils, and my mind was screaming for me to run, buck, kick out at the fire—anything I could do to fight my terror. Then May's familiar scent reached me, and that calmed me a little. I allowed her to grab my halter and lead me outside, where I took a breath of fresh air.

She left me there and hobbled quickly back

into the barn on her bad leg. I heard her shouting, and a few seconds later Coal burst out beside me, heaving and wild-eyed. May popped out and grabbed my halter again, leading me a little farther away from the barn.

"Hurry," she said breathlessly. "I'll need to go back for the sheep. . . ."

At that moment, a small, furry shape raced past—one of the dogs, soon followed by the other. There was a shout, and Gerrit came into view through the smoke, running in his nightclothes. He spotted May at my head and skidded to a stop, looking surprised.

"The sheep!" May cried before the old man could speak. "They're still in there!"

Gerrit nodded and whistled for the dogs. They appeared at his side, the smaller one following him into the barn without hesitation, though the larger dog danced around outside for a moment before diving in as well.

I didn't see what happened after that; the smoke was too thick, and flames were beginning to lick at the roof. May was tugging on my halter again, pulling me along toward the pasture gate.

Coal! I cried, not seeing my companion following. *Where are you?*

He whinnied back, sounding frightened. May heard him, too. She glanced around and spotted him huddled along the barn's outside wall, shaking with fear.

"Come on, big boy!" she cried. "Oh, Luna— why isn't he running away?"

I knew why, for I was battling the same feelings

myself. This barn was our home. Being so scared, it was tempting to run back inside, where we'd always been safe and snug.

But I shook off the feeling, whinnying to Coal again. *We must get to the pasture*, I told him.

Yes. He took a few slow steps toward me. *The pasture.*

Just then I heard Gerrit shouting and the dogs barking. A second later the sheep came pouring from the barn, out of their minds with terror. They raced around the farmyard, jumping this way and that and crashing into one another. A small ewe bounced off my hocks, bleating *Hot! Smoke! Scared, scared!* over and over again.

The eldest ewe circled all the way back around, heading for the barn door. *This way, this way!* she bleated frantically.

The others obeyed, shoving and bumping against one another as they tried to get back inside, nearly trampling Gerrit in the process. He leaped aside, and the dogs went to work, nipping and growling as they forced the sheep to turn once again.

"Gerrit!" A man and a teenage boy appeared out of the darkness—neighbors. "Where are you?"

"Thank God!" Gerrit exclaimed. "The sheep—I can't get them away from the barn."

"We have to help," May told me.

I'd nearly forgotten she was there. She pulled me along to the stone water trough and clambered clumsily onto the edge. I wasn't sure what she was doing at first.

Then she grabbed a chunk of my long, thick mane. "Hold still, Luna," she warned.

A second later I felt her small weight settle across my back. Gerrit never rode, but the boys at my birth farm had taught me about being ridden, and Kai occasionally jumped on bareback to ride me out and check the fences.

"Let's go, Luna." May pressed her small leg against my side, and her weight leaned along with it. I understood she wanted me to turn.

Having May on my back helped settle me further. I focused on what she wanted, walking toward the burning barn. I slowed as we neared it, but May pushed me forward.

"We have to get behind the sheep," she said.

After that, I did my best to forget about the fire and do as she asked. We circled behind the flock, helping the dogs, Gerrit, and the older neighbor to press them toward the pasture gate.

Meanwhile, out of the corner of my eye, I saw the teenage neighbor dive into the barn, appearing a moment later with his arms full of terrified chickens, which he tossed over the farmyard wall. I could hear them squawking with alarm over there but paid them little mind.

As we moved the sheep, more shouts came from nearby. Humans appeared from every direction. I recognized most of them as the residents of nearby farms and houses.

Then several oddly dressed men and boys rushed in from the direction of the pasture. They shouted to the others, and May gasped.

"It's my family," she whispered, clinging more tightly to my neck. "I can't let them see me."

But the circus men didn't spare a glance for me—or the small figure on my back. They raced past, joining the rest of the humans who were trying to beat back the flames with shirts or feed sacks. Some scooped water from the trough to pour on the ground nearby to keep the fire from spreading.

Just then a young sheep jumped off to the side, and I turned to block it before May could react. The sheep joined the rest of the flock, which finally seemed to be moving in the right direction. Coal was caught before them, and in the end he broke into a majestic, high-stepping trot through the pasture gate. The sheep followed him, running across the grass with loud bleats of fear.

5

Gerrit's Gift

By the time the local fire brigade finally arrived, the barn was little more than embers. May was still on my back, watching over the pasture fence.

"Oh, Luna," she whispered, twisting her fingers in my mane. "This is terrible. But I'm so glad you're safe."

Gerrit appeared suddenly beside us. Now that the fire was dying out, it was dark in the pasture.

"Hello, young one," Gerrit said, peering up at May. "I don't know where you came from, but thank you—it seems you saved my animals. Do you know how the fire started?"

"Yes," May said softly. "Two young men—they came in and stole your things. Then they set the barn afire, planning to blame my . . . my . . ." She glanced toward the circus tent, barely visible in the moonlight across the meadow.

The old man followed her gaze. "Yes, I suspected as much," he murmured. He smiled kindly. "You're with the circus?"

May nodded. "I didn't mean any harm," she said. "I just liked to visit Luna." She stroked my neck, then slid to the ground. She landed awkwardly, stumbling on her bad foot, and Gerrit put out a hand to steady her.

Then he glanced at me. "You call her Luna, eh?" Gerrit regarded me with interest before returning his attention to May. "Could you describe these young men?"

May spoke quickly, telling him all she'd seen. Soon Gerrit was nodding, his eyes sadder than ever.

"I know the pair you mean," he said. "Trouble-makers since they were boys, those two."

"Which two?" Another man hurried over just in time to hear him. He glanced at May. "Who's this?"

"Never mind her." Gerrit sighed. "It sounds as if Eilert and Joris are up to no good again. . . ."

There was much more talking after that,

though I had responded to my rumbling stomach and turned my attention to grazing. I was only vaguely aware that more people had gathered in the pasture, though I did lift my head when some of the men started shouting at one another.

"How dare you accuse us of setting this fire?" The man who'd spoken, one of the circus folk, was tall and slender. He had sleek dark hair, flashing brown eyes, and the air of a leader.

One of Gerrit's neighbors glared at him. "How dare *you* accuse my son?" he exclaimed. "He's a good boy."

Another neighbor snorted. "Are you certain of that, Pitter?"

May plucked at the tall man's sleeve. "Daddy, please," she said. "We should just go."

"Yes, perhaps we should," another man from

the circus group said. His features resembled the tall man's, though he was shorter and broader of shoulder, with a gruff voice. "Come, Lionel. Let the locals work this out on their own. We'll be gone in the morning in any case; it's no concern of ours."

"Yeah," one of the younger circus men muttered. "Nice way of thanking us for helping put out the fire."

"I do thank you, son," Gerrit told him. "Most sincerely. And I especially thank young May, here." He turned toward her. "If not for her, all my animals would have been lost."

May's father glanced at her. "Is that right?" he said. "Exactly what were you doing over here at this hour, May?"

"Maybe *she* set the fire," Pitter said, though he was quickly shouted down by the other neighbors.

"I . . . I just went for a walk," May said. "It was hot, and I couldn't sleep."

"However she came to be here, I'm glad she was," Gerrit put in. "And to thank her, I'd like to offer her a gift." He put a hand on my shoulder. "You seem to have taken to, er, Luna here. And I have little use for a second horse. I want you to have her."

May gasped. "You're giving me Luna?" she cried. "Really?"

Gerrit smiled. "Yes. I can tell you two are meant to be together."

"What?" May's father blurted out. "But we don't need—"

The shorter man cut him off. "Thank you, sir," he said. "We'll be going now."

"Yes, thank you, thank you!" May's eyes were shining as she looked at me.

May took my lead rope, and she and I followed

along behind the others. I flicked an ear back toward Gerrit; a few of the neighbors were grumbling suspiciously, though most were already discussing mounting a search for the two youths.

Then Coal noticed I was leaving. Letting out a snort, he trotted to catch up.

Where are you going? he asked.

With May, I responded.

When we reached the far end of the pasture, the younger men lifted a few boards out of the way to lead me through, while the others shooed Coal away. Soon the boards were back in place and Coal was watching over the fence as I moved away.

More people awaited us near the tent. There were a number of women, along with half a dozen children and an elderly man. The dogs I'd seen from a distance were with them. Nearby were the other horses. A few of them snorted curiously as I came closer.

"Oh, May!" A woman rushed forward, grabbing May in her arms. "When the fire woke us and we realized you were missing . . ."

"I'm all right, Mama." May's voice was muffled by her mother's embrace.

Another girl hugged May next. She was a little older than May, with pale eyes and wavy brown hair that fell softly around her shoulders. "Yes, we were terribly worried, May!"

"You don't need to worry so much about me, Minerva." May pulled away from her sister quickly. "I can take care of myself."

The old man stepped forward to peer at me,

leaning heavily on a cane. "What happened? And where did this horse come from?"

In a rush of words, May and the men told the story of the fire. However, I hardly heard their talk; I was busy sniffing the air around me. Over the past few days I'd grown accustomed to the faint, odd smell that Coal and I had noticed on the first day. But it was much stronger here and made me a little uneasy. I shifted my weight, turning my head this way and that as I tried to figure out where the odor could be coming from.

"Easy there, big girl." The broad-shouldered man was still holding my halter. "Stand still, that's a good girl."

"Oh, Uncle Claude," the older girl said. "Luna's just nervous, that's all."

May's mother glanced at the pale horses. "All the animals are nervous from smelling the fire."

"Luna wasn't scared at all," May said. "She helped rescue the other animals."

"Did she, now?" May's father, Lionel, glanced at me and sighed. "That may be true. But what are we going to do with another horse?"

"And an untrained one at that," Claude added.

"I can train her," May said. "She's smart— she'll learn fast."

One of the younger boys shouted with laughter. "You? But you don't even ride!"

"Hugo!" May's mother chided. "That's enough."

Meanwhile, May's sister, Minerva, stepped closer, running a gentle hand down my face and neck. "She's beautiful," she said. "I bet audiences would love her."

"Do you think so?" Her mother studied me with new interest. "I suppose she is different, with the long mane and all."

"We could braid roses into it," Minerva said. "Wouldn't that be pretty, May?"

"Pretty doesn't pay for hay," their father said with a frown. "We have enough horses. I say we drop her off in her home field on our way out of town in the morning."

"What?" May cried. "Daddy, no!"

"Let's not be hasty, Lionel," Claude said thoughtfully. "Minerva has a point. This is an impressive-looking beast, and we can probably sell her for a nice sum in one of the cities. It would be foolish to give her back."

"We can't sell her," May said. "She's mine!"

Her mother petted her head. "It's all right, May. We'll work it out. Now let's get you to bed—you must be exhausted."

"In a moment," May said. "I want to help get Luna settled."

"Your uncle can take care of that," Minerva cooed. "Come, now."

May's lower lip jutted out, and she frowned. But she allowed her mother and sister to lead her toward the cluster of trailers and tents nearby, while Claude led me in the other direction, toward the other horses. One of the older boys walked with us.

At first my attention was on the horses who were to be my new herd. As we drew closer, however, the other scent—the strange, wild, unknown one—became stronger. Finally we passed a wagon with a large iron cage set upon it, and there I encountered the source of the scent.

It was an animal, but one I'd never seen before—large, brown, shaggy, with long claws and a doglike face. But I knew it was no dog. I stopped short, raising my head as high as it would go for a better look.

"Come on, now." Claude tugged on my halter.

"She's looking at the bear, Pa," the older boy said.

"Well, she'll have to get used to him." Claude tugged again. "At least for as long as she's with us."

I planted my feet, not willing to move past the beast until I'd convinced myself it wouldn't hurt me. Meanwhile, the other horses were watching me. One of them, a pretty dapple-gray mare, let out a snort.

"It's all right," she called to me. "He's a bear. He travels with us, and he's harmless."

A bear. I'd never heard of such a creature. But the other horses had been grazing quite close to the bear's cage, seemingly without fear.

I lowered my head, stepping forward as Claude urged me on. Keeping a wary eye on the bear, I joined my new herd.

The Tent

Over the next few days, I learned much more about my new life as a circus horse. Very early that first morning, I was hitched to a heavy wagon beside one of the other horses, a stout palomino gelding named Midas. The rest of the horses went to work, too, although the smallest—the delicate dapple-gray mare with an arched neck—walked beside one of the wagons with the dogs.

We traveled all day, passing through a series of towns and villages before stopping in a field for the night. Claude seemed pleased with my work as he unhitched me.

"This one is strong and willing, at least," he told Lionel, who was passing by carrying a bale of hay.

Lionel surveyed me. "Yes, but we need a performer, not a plow horse."

Claude shrugged. "I suppose you're right. Still, having her here gave Arabia a rest, at least."

My muscles were tired after the long journey. I was looking forward to rest and food but was disappointed to find that we horses had only a small area of sparse grass to nibble on, with some dry hay to make up the rest of our meal.

Never mind, Midas said, noticing my reaction. *Sometimes we have lots of grass, and at other times none.*

The pretty dapple gray lifted her head. *Yes. The next place might be better.*

The other five horses had welcomed me, though I could tell they found my size and dark coat strange. My favorite among them was the dapple-gray mare, who was named Arabia. Apart from Midas, the other three were all white-gray. There were two geldings, King and Jasper, and an older mare known as Fancy. They told me more about this strange new world I'd joined, explaining that the circus was a form of human entertainment. May's family traveled all across the land, performing for audiences in tiny hamlets and big cities alike.

Her father, Lionel, was the ringmaster. He was in charge of the show and directed all that happened. May's mother was an aerialist.

I've seen her perform, Arabia said. *She twirls through the air like a bird!*

The horses themselves were part of the act. Uncle Claude had trained them all to perform various feats. Arabia was the star of the show, cantering gracefully around the ring night after night as Minerva did flips and jumps upon her back.

The rest of the family took part in the show, too. May's brothers and cousins made up the clown troupe; Claude's wife had trained the dogs to dance on command; another aunt and uncle walked on a high wire; various other cousins worked with the bear or did other things. It was difficult to keep track of all that went into the circus—it certainly seemed much more complicated than Gerrit's humble farm!

I might have been distressed by all these changes if not for May's quiet, loving presence. Having her around made everything easier.

Our first morning in our new location, she came to see me early. "Good morning, Luna," she said, feeding me a bite of carrot. "Uncle Claude says he'll begin your training today."

I crunched the sweet carrot, enjoying the treat. As May untangled a knot in my mane, Claude hurried over with Minerva at his heels.

"All right, I don't have much time," Claude said briskly. "Let's see what this horse can do."

He slipped a bridle on my head and then tossed Minerva onto my bare back. She was almost as light as May, though her legs gripped me more strongly. She rode me around the field at a walk, trot, and canter.

"Very nice," Claude said. "Flashy trot, eh? See what she does if you stand up."

I felt Minerva pulling her legs up. Soon her feet pressed into my back, and her weight shifted. It felt odd, so I stopped.

"Come along, girl." Claude put a hand on the rein. "Keep going."

I hesitated, worried that Minerva would become unbalanced. But she felt steady, so I stepped off again, though more slowly. This seemed to please all the humans, and they praised me with happy voices.

Then someone called for Claude to come help with the tent, and he hurried off. "See to the tack, Minerva," he called over his shoulder as he went.

As soon as he'd disappeared, May came forward and reached for the bridle. "It's all right, May, I've got it," Minerva said kindly.

"I can help," May said. "I may have a bad foot, but I'm not completely useless, you know."

"Oh, May." Minerva trilled out a laugh. "Nobody thinks you're useless. We just want to keep you safe." She quickly unbuckled the bridle and pulled it off.

"Do you think we'll be able to keep Luna?" May asked.

"I hope so," Minerva replied lightly. "I really like her."

"I hope so, too." May gazed at me, biting her lower lip. "I couldn't stand it if they sold her."

"Well, let's leave her to rest," Minerva said. "We'll just have to wait and see what happens."

By that afternoon, the tent was standing. It looked much larger than it had from a distance in my old pasture. I kept one eye on it as I nibbled my hay that afternoon.

What is it for, the tent? I asked the others.

Arabia looked up. *Why, it's where we do the shows,* she said.

I didn't understand what she meant. Before I could ask, Uncle Claude and Minerva hurried over.

"Should we wait for May?" Minerva asked. "Mother's washing her hair."

"No, it's better she's not underfoot," Claude said. "If the horse panics, I don't want poor May getting run over."

He clipped a lead rope to my halter and led me away from the others. I walked obediently until we were just a few steps from the tent. There was an opening in the fabric, and all I could see within was darkness. I stopped short, raising my head and pricking my ears at it.

"Come along, Luna," Claude said. "We're just going to look inside."

I ignored him, still worried by that dark space. He tugged impatiently on the rope, then whacked my rump with the flat of his hand. That only made me back up a step. If he was so upset, could there be a reason to be nervous?

"Stop, Uncle Claude!" Minerva exclaimed. "You're just scaring her more. Here, let me try."

Claude cursed, then tossed her the lead rope. "Be my guest," he growled, backing off a few paces.

Minerva came to my head, petting me and coaxing me forward in a sweet voice. I cocked an ear in her direction, keeping the other trained on the tent. Gradually I realized that Minerva didn't seem anxious at all. Could it be that the dark place was safe?

I took a cautious step forward, and then another. "Good girl!" Minerva cried. "What a brave horse."

By now I could see the cavernous space within the tent. It was dim and shadowy. Every touch of breeze made the tent shake and shimmer and the shadows dance.

Suddenly I heard a familiar voice calling my name. A moment later May appeared, hobbling along quickly with the help of her cane.

"Oh! There you are, Luna!" she exclaimed. She glanced at Minerva and Claude. "What's going on?"

"She's scared of the tent." Claude still sounded impatient. "We don't have all day. If she won't go in, she'll never make a circus horse."

"Let me try," May said. "Please? I know I can get her to go in."

"Absolutely not," Claude said. "Stay well away in case she bolts."

"She won't bolt." May stepped forward into

the dark entrance. "Here, Luna! Come on, girl—
come to me."

I relaxed at the sight of her, the sound of her
voice. Taking a step forward, I stretched my nose

toward her. Minerva came along with me, still holding my lead. When we neared, May took a step back. Once again, I stepped forward.

Another step, and another. Before I knew it, we were inside the tent. For a moment I was nervous. But when May praised me and petted me, I relaxed again. Being with her was good. It didn't matter where.

7

Training

After that, either Minerva or Uncle Claude rode me nearly every day, sometimes in the usual way and sometimes standing or crouching upon my back. They taught me different, lighter commands for the various gaits and maneuvers. I liked Minerva well enough and was obedient to all she asked of me, although Claude could be abrupt—sometimes his manner distracted me from what he was asking and I would stop what I was doing entirely. That only made him impatient, which made things more confusing. He left more and more of my training to Minerva.

May often came to watch, though the others insisted she stay well back out of the way. I wasn't sure why, since May also came to see me every night, just as she had at Gerrit's farm. During those times, she was the one who rode me—cautiously at first, just circling the grazing area at a walk. But each night, she did a little more. We trotted, then cantered our circles. Finally May began doing some of the things Minerva did during the day—crouching and standing on my back. Whatever troubled her gait on the ground seemed not to bother her while riding; she was nearly as graceful as Minerva when it came to turning about and balancing in odd positions up there.

One night she rode me right up to the tent entrance and then inside. I was nervous at first, but having May on my back helped me be brave. After a couple of visits, the tent became familiar rather than frightening. Going inside was no different from going into Gerrit's barn.

During all this, the circus moved twice more, the second time settling in a grassy field just outside a large town. *We've been here before,* Midas told me as one of May's cousins unhitched us. *We'll probably stay awhile.*

Yes, Fancy agreed. *Lots of people means lots of shows.*

I wasn't sorry to hear it, since the grazing here was good. Stuffing my mouth with sweet grass, I barely looked up as the humans erected the tent nearby.

May was combing out my feathers when her father came to bring us water. "We'll have to make a decision about the mare soon, May," Lionel warned as he poured his bucket into our trough. "If Claude doesn't think she's going to work out, this would be a good place to sell her."

"But Luna's been learning so fast!" May exclaimed. "Even Uncle Claude says so."

"Yes, he mentioned that she's made some progress." Lionel patted me on the neck, looking me over. "But he hasn't decided what to do about her yet."

May seemed worried for the rest of the day, and that evening she spent even longer than usual on my training, asking me to do nearly everything we'd practiced. After we'd finished, she once again rode me into the tent. The humans had set up a low wooden wall forming a circle in the center, and May asked me to canter around inside it several times.

Finally she stopped in the center, rubbing my withers. "We have to show Uncle Claude that you can be a circus horse," she told me. "I suggested he try taking you into the tent again, but he only said it will be different with a crowd inside, and he's afraid you'd be too nervous." She glanced around the vast space, empty except for some wooden seats, wires, and other strange objects. "Oh! But that gives me an idea. . . ."

* * *

The next day, all the humans were busier than ever. I'd already learned what this meant—there would be a show that evening. I watched between mouthfuls of grass as the other horses were brushed, their hooves polished, and flowers and ribbons woven into their manes and tails.

Soon people from the town began trickling into the tent. From where I was tied near the wagons, I could see May sitting at a table outside with one of her aunts, exchanging bits of paper with the visitors as they went inside.

Finally the tent flap fell shut. I heard Lionel's booming voice inside welcoming the audience to the show. After that I stopped paying attention, focusing instead on the grass. Most of the other horses had gone, waiting their turns near the tent. But Jasper had the night off and grazed with me.

Then May appeared and untied me. "Come with me, Luna," she whispered, her voice quavering slightly.

She led me toward the tent. I hesitated as we drew closer; there was a different feeling about the place now, full of people and excitement. But at May's gentle urging, I moved forward again.

May lifted the flap, hooking it out of the way so we could look in.

What a sight it was! Arabia was cantering around the edge of the ring while Minerva stood on her back doing flips and handstands. Claude stood in the center with a long whip, while Lionel watched from nearby, dressed in a splendid red coat. The ring was surrounded by humans of all

ages, many of them letting out shouts, cheers, and laughter as they watched the show.

I pricked my ears, taking it all in. May spoke
soothingly to me, so I wasn't afraid.

After a moment, she asked me again to step forward. I did, and we were soon inside the tent.

A boy sitting on one of the wooden benches nearby looked over. "Mama, look at the big black horse!" he cried.

His shrill voice brought attention from others. Soon people all over the tent were craning their necks for a look at me.

Claude noticed, peering in my direction. For a second he looked annoyed.

"When do we see that black one go?" a man shouted.

Lionel stepped forward. "This is our latest addition, a fine mare from Holland," he boomed out. "Who would like to see the Marvelous Minerva ride this fiery beast?"

There were shouts of excitement. Before I

knew what was happening, Claude pulled the rope from May's hand and led me into the ring. Minerva dismounted from Arabia and handed her to one of the clowns. Then she vaulted onto my back and waved to the cheering crowd.

"Come along, Luna," Claude said with a cluck.

I hesitated, unnerved by the din of cheers and shouting, the waving arms and eager faces surrounding me. But Arabia gave me a snort of encouragement from where she stood just outside the ring, held by one of May's cousins. And when I looked for May, I saw her smiling at me. That gave me courage to walk on beside Claude.

We circled the ring at a steady walk. Halfway around, a small child tossed a scrap of bright fabric at my feet, which startled me so that I shied to one side.

"Easy there, big girl," Claude said loudly as Minerva put a hand on my neck to keep her balance.

Once again, I looked at May. She was still there. I kept walking, and we soon reached her end of the ring again. The crowd cheered loudly as Minerva slid down and landed beside me with a flourish. I heard Lionel's voice booming out something about the "magnificent Friesian horse" as Claude led me out of the tent.

May hobbled along beside us. "Well?" she demanded as we emerged into the warm twilight of the evening. "She did wonderfully, didn't she? And the crowd loved her!"

"That they did," Claude admitted. "I suppose she does cut a fine picture out there." He rubbed

his chin and studied me. "If we can get her spook-iness under control . . ."

"Oh, Uncle!" May laughed. "She only jumped when something fell under her feet. Even Fancy would do the same!"

"Hmm." Claude gave me a pat. "Well, we'll see. But perhaps your Luna will make a circus horse after all."

Circus Horse

After that night, Claude seemed to have gained enthusiasm for my training. He and Minerva worked with me as often as they could, and May's nighttime sessions continued as well. I performed well for the others, but it was with May that I truly enjoyed my work.

May gained in confidence with every passing night. Gradually she began doing some of the more difficult tricks Minerva performed in the ring, and new ones, too—balancing on her good foot while twirling in a circle, hanging off my side, and more. Some nights we worked nearly until dawn, though May always crept back into her sleeping wagon before the others awoke.

We moved several more times, stopping at a series of hamlets and country villages, where the circus would perform a few shows before moving on. Finally we left the farmland for a more densely populated area, settling along a picturesque riverbank outside the largest town we'd visited yet.

It was there that it came time for my debut as an official part of the show. May and Minerva spent all afternoon scrubbing my black coat to a shine and combing out my mane, tail, and feathers. Then May painted something foul-smelling and shiny on my hooves, while her sister braided silvery ribbons into my mane and tail.

"Oh, Luna." Minerva stepped back to survey me. "You look beautiful!"

"She's always beautiful." May's eyes shone with pride.

Just before showtime, Claude and one of the cousins led me and Arabia to a spot outside the tent's rear entrance. Minerva had disappeared but May walked beside me, keeping a hand on my side. From inside the tent, I could hear the crowd roaring with laughter.

The clown troupe is performing first tonight, Arabia told me. *Humans always react that way to their antics.*

Then Minerva reappeared, running lightly over the grass. She'd changed into her show outfit, a silvery tutu with lots of sparkles that caught the light. "Ready, Luna?" she exclaimed. "Let's go!"

She vaulted onto my back and picked up the reins, guiding me away from May and into the tent. One of her cousins was leading Arabia behind me, though she stopped outside the ring while I continued in. I paused for a moment, looking back. May had entered and was standing near the entrance watching me. Seeing her made me feel I could do anything.

"And now, our magnificent Friesian horse, the stupendous Luna!" Lionel shouted as the crowd cheered.

Minerva asked me to canter, and I obeyed. Claude stood in the center of the ring holding his whip, which he occasionally waggled in my direction. I paid little attention to him, knowing my job already. I cantered steadily around the outside of the ring while Minerva stood and waved her arms to oohs and aahs from the audience.

The performance lasted only a few minutes.

It ended when Arabia trotted into the ring, and Minerva guided me toward her. "Steady, girl," she said—and then leaped gracefully off my back and onto the other mare's.

We'd practiced that move many times. The difference this time was the gasp and shout from the crowd, which made me jump and plant my feet, startled. But by then, Arabia was cantering away, all eyes on Minerva as she began more elaborate acrobatics upon the gray mare's back.

One of the cousins ran in, grabbed my bridle, and led me out. May was waiting, smiling from ear to ear.

"Oh, Luna," she said, hugging me. "You were wonderful—just as I knew you would be!"

* * *

Later that night, the entire family gathered in the field outside the wagons, where May was taking the ribbons out of my mane as I grazed with the other horses. All the humans were still excited; I could feel the happy energy radiating from them as they talked. Even Grandfather hobbled out to join in, leaning heavily on his cane.

"I have to admit, May—your Luna was a big hit tonight," Lionel said.

One of May's aunts nodded. "People stopped after the show to ask about her. There aren't many horses like her in these parts."

"We should put her on the posters," someone said. "She could be a draw."

"Yes," Claude agreed. "People across Europe are already talking about our act, thanks to

Minerva. We need to keep up the momentum, and this mare can only help with that."

"Especially if you let her do more," May spoke up. "All Min did tonight was a couple of waves and turns. Luna can do more than that."

"We'll see." Claude sounded distracted. "For now it's enough for her to appear at all. People love seeing that big black horse with the flowing hair—they don't even care about tricks." He shrugged. "Besides, the other horses are steadier. Did you see her spook?"

"She's still getting used to things," May said. "Don't you remember how much Jasper jumped around when he first came?"

"It's all right, May," Minerva said. "Everyone loved Luna. That's what you wanted, right? Now she can stay with us!"

"Yes, but . . . ," May began.

The others didn't hear her. They were already chattering on, still excited about the successful show. May turned away to hug me, burying her face in my neck.

"I don't care what they say, Luna," she murmured beneath the swell of chatter around us. "You're the best circus horse ever!"

We did several more shows in the large town, then moved on again. Each night, Minerva rode me into the ring and did the same series of easy tricks while the crowd cheered; then she switched to one of the other horses for the rest of her act. And each night when we finished, I felt May's frustration grow.

"If you don't want to do more with Luna,

maybe *I* should ride her in the show!" she blurted out one fine evening after a performance in a peaceful little town near a lake.

Minerva laughed and ruffled her hair. "Don't even joke about that in front of Mother," she said. "You know how she worries about you." She gave me a pat and hurried off.

May gnashed her teeth. "None of them believe I can do anything, Luna," she said. "I wish I could show them it's not true." She paused for a moment, then shook her head. "But if they find out I've been riding at night, they might make me stop. Then I'll really have no reason to stay."

Sensing that she was upset, I nuzzled her shoulder. She reached up and wrapped her arms around my nose, hugging my head.

"Oh, Luna." Now her voice was choked with

tears. "Maybe I had the right idea to run away. If things don't change . . ." She paused again, for longer this time, then continued. "If things don't change soon, I should just take you and run away for real this time. After all, nobody here *really* appreciates either one of us!"

Flashbacks

Over the next several months, we never stopped traveling. However, as time passed, we did begin to remain in each location longer and longer— sometimes for more than a week at a time. The circus's fame was growing, and the crowds were coming from farther away to see the marvelous equestrian spectacle and other acts. This clearly pleased Lionel, Claude, and the other humans. They were in jolly moods most of the time, and Claude even started slipping me bits of carrot or other treats now and then, calling me his "star attraction."

May still talked about running away. But so far she seemed willing to watch me in the ring each evening and ride me beneath the stars after everyone else had gone to sleep. And I was content with that, too.

One fine autumn afternoon, we stopped in a field outside a very large town. Something about the smells and trees and wildlife there seemed oddly familiar, though I didn't waste much time thinking about it as I settled down to enjoy the sweet late-season grass alongside the other horses.

There was the usual flurry of unloading and such, though the tent lay ignored on the ground for the moment. When May came to hand-graze me a little later, I was happy to see her.

"Do you recognize where we are, Luna?" May said as we wandered away from the others. "We crossed over from Germany yesterday and now we're in Groningen—we've come back around nearly to your old home. It's only a couple of days' ride from here."

Just then Minerva came running, hair flying and her expression excited. "May! May!" she cried. "You'll never guess what's happened—the mayor wants to meet us!"

"What?" May said.

"The mayor of Groningen," Minerva explained, clapping her hands and dancing about.

"We're so famous now that he's invited us to a special dinner in our honor! Isn't that wonderful?"

"I suppose so," May said in a small voice. "Are you sure I'm invited? After all, I'm not in the show."

Minerva shook her head impatiently. "Of course—we're all invited. Grandpa's staying behind to keep an eye on things, but the rest of us will leave in a few minutes. Now hurry—we need to get dressed in our finest clothes!" Grabbing May by the hand, she dragged her off, barely allowing her time to secure me with the other horses.

A little while later, the family left, walking off toward the town lights twinkling in the distance. I looked for May's familiar figure among the group but didn't see her.

I soon found out why. After a few minutes, May emerged from one of the trailers. Looking around carefully, she hurried toward me, trailed by one of the dogs.

She rubbed my face. "I told them I was sick so I could stay behind with Grandpa," she whispered. "He's already asleep, so I'll have extra time with you tonight. We'll just have to listen for the rest of the family returning. . . ."

Then she was slipping on my bridle. Darkness was coming earlier each night as the cold season neared, but darkness didn't bother me. As May climbed onto my back from atop a fallen log, the dog barked and leaped around my forefeet.

"Hush!" May whispered. When the dog kept barking, she slid down and grabbed it, carrying it over to the trailer where the other dogs were sleeping, and shutting it inside. "There," she said when she returned. "Grandpa left him out as a guard, but we don't need him getting in our way."

She led me to the log and climbed aboard again, and we began, practicing the moves we'd nearly perfected over the past few months. I was light on my feet, and May was like a feather on my back. We moved together almost as one being. I supposed it was similar to what the humans called dancing, the special ways the dogs and the bear moved when their turns came in the ring.

We were trotting in a circle when a new scent drifted into my nostrils. My gait faltered slightly. Why did it seem familiar? Was it just another type of bird or hare from my homeland, one I'd forgotten during my time away?

But no—this scent wasn't an animal. It was

humans—ones I knew. Ones who made me feel uneasy.

I stopped, raising my head to look around. "What is it, Luna?" May asked, kicking at my sides to ask me to walk on. "Why did you stop?"

For once I ignored her, staying where I was. I'd located the source of the scent—it was coming from a wooded area on one side of the field. Pricking my ears that way, I heard rough voices.

The moon was rising by now, but it was little more than a sliver, casting only the faintest silvery light. Still, my keen eyes made out two shapes creeping across the meadow toward the wagons and trailers.

I didn't know if May could see them. But by now she'd heard them. She let out a gasp as a guffaw came from that direction.

"Oh no," she whispered, clinging to my neck. "It can't be—I think it's those two ruffians who burned down your barn!"

She was right. Those very same two youths were creeping across the field in the direction of the circus's wagons and trailers, which were lit by a few oil lamps. The young men hadn't seen us yet; we were hidden by the darkness, my black coat the perfect camouflage. Still, I could feel May's heart beating faster than usual as she clung to me.

"What are we going to do?" she whispered. "Why are they here?"

The youths were talking to each other in loud, gruff whispers. "I can't believe it's the same circus," one of them was saying. "They should've known better than to show their faces where we'd find 'em!"

The other one chuckled, though there was little humor in the sound. "I'm glad they didn't," he said. "They ruined our lives, turned us into wanted criminals. Now's our chance to make them pay!"

"Yeah." His friend sounded pleased. "I just saw them all prance into the mayor's house. Hard to believe the mayor would want to entertain common circus folk! But I'd guess they'll be there awhile."

"And by the time they get back," the other finished, "their precious circus will be nothing but a pile of ash."

At that, both youths burst into snorts of laughter. "Come, let's not waste any time, then," the first youth said at last.

They hurried forward. There was a flare and a whiff of smoke as one of them lit a match. Fancy and King let out uneasy snorts from somewhere in the darkness. I felt my own heart race as the smell of fire brought back the terrifying night in my burning barn.

May was still trembling on my back, but then I felt something shift in her manner. Sitting up straight, she kicked me forward, and this time I obeyed.

My hoofbeats alerted the youths, and they spun to face us. "Who's there?" one yelped, holding up his small flame.

"Relax—it's just a horse," the other said.

"No, I'm here, too," May said loudly. "And you'd better stop right now!"

Her legs were still pressing against my sides, so I kept moving forward. The youths stared at me, startled.

"Who's there?" one of them blurted out again. "A talking horse?"

The other was peering up at May. "Don't be daft—it's just a little girl," he said with a sneer. "Clear off, miss, or you'll be sorry."

"You're the ones who should clear off," May cried. "Go away and leave us alone!"

"Says who?" the first youth muttered. But I was still coming at him, and he took a step back, eyeing me warily. "Stop your horse before it runs me over."

"No," May said, giving me another nudge with her heel. This time both youths backed away.

"Stop right now!" one of them shouted.

Suddenly there came the sound of one of the trailer doors opening. "Who's out there?" Grandpa's quavery voice called.

"Grandpa! Let the dogs out!" May hollered. "There are bad men out here!"

"May? That you?" The old man sounded surprised. But a moment later the dogs burst out of their trailer, barking wildly as they raced toward us, yapping and snarling around the youths' legs.

"Shoo, you mutts!" one of the youths exclaimed.

"Just kick 'em away," his friend said. "They're silly circus dogs."

He aimed a kick at the smallest dog. Luckily she dodged in time, returning a second later to nip at the youth's pant leg.

Then I heard the sound of another door opening, this one with the screeching scrape of a metal latch. The two troublemakers turned toward the sound and gasped.

"Look out, mate!" one exclaimed. "What is that thing?"

"A bear!" his friend cried in a voice made shrill with terror. "I'm getting out of here!"

"Oh no, you're not." May steered me over to block their way. I was keeping one wary eye on the bear, who was lumbering toward us, sniffing the air. But I'd grown accustomed to his scent and presence over the past few months and resisted the urge to bolt away. May seemed to hold no fear of the bear at all, and that gave me courage.

Grandpa hurried after the bear, waving his cane. He noticed the burning corner of the wagon and stopped just long enough to smother it with his hat. "What are you doing out here, May? Who are these scoundrels?"

"They set the fire in Luna's barn back in

Friesland," May replied. "And now they want to set fire to the circus!"

"Do they, now?" Grandpa's voice went grim. "Brutus, sic 'em!" He waved his cane at the bear, who had stopped to sniff at a stray pile of manure.

Brutus looked up at the sound of his name and let out a loud roar. I knew from what the other horses had told me, and from hearing the sound myself coming from within the tent, that this was part of the act. The bear had been trained to respond that way to the phrase "Brutus, sic 'em."

But the youths didn't know that. Yelping with fear, they dove beneath one of the wagons. "We confess!" one cried. "Just call off that monster!"

Grandpa stepped forward, poking at a youth's leg with his cane. Then he squinted up at May. An expression of surprise crossed his face.

"You're riding, child," he said. "But I thought—
Well, never mind. Ride off to town and fetch the
others, then, would you? The local police will
want to have a word with these two."

"But what if they try to hurt you?" May asked.

Grandpa chuckled. "Don't worry, they won't be coming out as long as Brutus is here with me. Now go!"

A New Life

As it happened, we had no need to ride all the way into town, for we encountered a pair of policemen halfway there. When May told them what had happened, one hurried off to find May's family, while the other accompanied us back to the circus to arrest the youths. We found them exactly where we'd left them, whimpering with fear as Brutus sniffed at their feet sticking out from beneath the wagon.

By the time the rest of the family returned, breathless and full of questions, May had slipped down from my back and was holding my reins while I grazed. Brutus was back in his cage, and the youths were off to the local jailhouse.

"Oh, May!" Her mother enveloped her in a hug. "You must have been so scared!"

"A little," May said. "But I was with Luna, so I knew I'd be all right."

"With Luna?" Her mother pulled back and glanced at me. "I thought you were ill in bed."

"Good thing she wasn't," Grandpa said,

hobbling over to rest a gnarled hand on May's shoulder. "She stopped those scoundrels from burning the whole circus to the ground."

"She did?" Claude looked impressed. "So our May is a hero."

"Of course she is," Minerva exclaimed. "And she deserves a reward!"

"That she does," Lionel agreed. "We owe you our livelihood, May. What can we do to thank you? A new dress? A fancy dinner?"

"There are some marvelous places to eat in this town," one of the aunts added.

May was shaking her head. "There's only one thing I want," she said softly, glancing at me.

"What's that?" Her father leaned closer. "Speak up, girl."

May cleared her throat. When she spoke

again, her voice was firmer and louder. "I said, there's only one thing I want," she told everyone. "I want to perform in the show."

Lionel looked surprised. "Perform? You?"

"Doing what?" a cousin asked.

"She could be a clown with us," May's little brother Oliver suggested. "She could sit in the wagon and squirt us with the hose."

"I don't want to be a clown," May said. "I want to ride in the equestrian show. I know Luna and I could do it if you only gave me a chance."

Her father was already shaking his head. "Out of the question," he said. "With your leg . . ."

"Her leg didn't hold her back when she rode Luna after those troublemakers," Grandpa put in.

"She was riding?" Now Lionel was starting to look angry. "May, I thought we were clear on this—I don't want you risking your safety by handling the horses. And certainly not by riding!"

"But, Daddy, I've been riding Luna every night, and she's never hurt me!" May protested.

"You have?" Minerva asked in surprise.

May nodded. "We can do lots of tricks," she told her sister, excitement creeping into her voice. "Some new ones, even."

"I think it's time for bed," May's mother said. "We can discuss how to handle this in the morning."

I lifted my head from the grass, sensing that the mood of the humans had shifted. Before, they'd been happy and excited. Now most of them were frowning, and May looked sad and anxious.

Then Minerva stepped forward and took my

reins from May's hand. Instead of leading me back toward the other horses, however, she stepped to my side.

"Hurry," she murmured to her sister. "You won't have long to prove yourself to them."

May's jaw dropped. "What?"

"I'll give you a leg up," Minerva whispered. "After that, it's up to you."

Still May hesitated, staring at her sister. Minerva gave her a gentle shove toward my shoulder.

"I know you're scared," she said. "If you're going to be a performer, you'll have to learn to swallow your fear and perform your best anyway."

Finally May seemed to wake up. She lifted her bad knee, and Minerva tossed her lightly onto my back.

"May!" her mother exclaimed. "What on earth—"

I was already moving, urged into a trot by May's legs. A moment later I slipped into a canter.

"May, stop that immediately!" Lionel cried.

"Wait," Grandpa said. "Look at her!"

I could sense May's nervousness, but a moment later I felt her stand on my back. The others watched with amazement as she began to perform all our familiar moves. In the beginning, her parents called out a few times for her to stop, but after a while their protests faded away.

Finally May brought me to a halt, out of breath. Nobody spoke for a moment as she stared at her family.

Then Uncle Claude started to applaud. "Brava, May," he said. "It seems we've been underestimating you all this time."

"And Luna too." Minerva sounded impressed. "She's amazing!"

"So can I ride in the show?" May asked. I felt her catch her breath and hold it as she awaited a response.

Her parents traded a long, anxious look. Finally Lionel nodded.

"We can give it a try, I suppose," he said. "Be ready tomorrow night."

The next evening, May shivered as we stood outside the tent waiting our turn. "I hope we can do this, Luna," she murmured, burying her fingers in my mane.

At that moment, a cousin opened the tent flap and gestured us inside. I trotted into the ring, ignoring the cheers and howls of the crowd. Focusing only on May, I awaited her commands.

And thus the performance began. I cantered steadily around the ring, just as I'd been taught. May stood upon my back, twirling and somer-saulting and dancing as she'd practiced every night for months. When she started to bobble while resting on her bad foot, I shifted my weight to the side until she caught her balance. The rest of the time, all I needed to do was keep my gait regular and steady, and May did the rest.

By the end, the crowd was cheering wildly. Minerva watched from Arabia's back nearby, grinning widely. Even Lionel couldn't resist applauding from his ringmaster's stand when his younger daughter took her bows.

A moment later, everyone gasped and then shouted with approval when May touched me on the shoulder in a certain way she'd taught me—and I took a bow, too, bending one foreleg and lowering my head toward the ground. We'd practiced that trick almost every night and I was proud to show it off.

Finally I trotted out of the ring, head held high, feeling May's happiness radiating through her body and into mine. I hardly remembered the old days in my quiet field anymore. For I was a circus horse now, and I loved my interesting new life with my favorite girl.

APPENDIX

MORE ABOUT THE FRIESIAN HORSE

Native to the Netherlands

Friesians have been bred in Friesland, a region of the Netherlands, for hundreds of years. It's the only breed of horse that originates in the Netherlands. Long ago, Friesians were used as warhorses and later as carriage horses and for farmwork. They were also used in trotting races, a popular pastime in the 1800s.

Back in Black

By the late nineteenth century, the Friesian breed had dwindled in numbers in its native land and elsewhere. Its blood had been diluted by crossbreeding, and the Friesian was in danger of dying out. But a group of fanciers took action, bringing the breed back stronger than ever. A Friesian is recognizable for its luxurious mane, tail, and feathers and for its black coat—no white is permitted except for a small star.

Horses in the Circus

Riders have performed tricks on horseback since ancient Roman times. But the origin of today's circus acts is a bit more recent. An Englishman named Philip Astley is known as the father of the modern circus thanks to his invention of the circus ring in the 1700s. He was also an equestrian, and horses and trick riding were the mainstay of his shows. In the 1930s, the Circus Strassburger started using Friesian horses in their performances. The breed is well suited to the job due to its steady temperament and impressive appearance.

Friesians Today

Today, the Friesian is a popular breed all over the world, featured in movies and advertising. Gentle and intelligent, they are used in a variety of riding and driving sports, from dressage to saddle seat to carriage driving. Breed fanciers swear by Friesians' affectionate temperament and inclination to bond with their owners, as well as their high-stepping trot and dramatic good looks.

ABOUT THE AUTHOR

Catherine Hapka has written more than 150 books for children and young adults, including many about horses. A lifelong horse lover, she rides several times a week and appreciates horses of all breeds. In addition to writing and riding, she enjoys all kinds of animals, reading, gardening, music, and travel. She lives on a small farm in Chester County, Pennsylvania, which she shares with a horse, three goats, a small flock of chickens, and too many cats.

ABOUT THE ILLUSTRATOR

Ruth Sanderson grew up with a love for horses. She has illustrated and retold many fairy tales and likes to feature horses in them whenever possible. Her book about a magical horse, *The Golden Mare, the Firebird, and the Magic Ring,* won the Texas Bluebonnet Award.

Ruth and her daughter have two horses, an Appaloosa named Thor and a quarter horse named Gabriel. She lives with her family in Massachusetts.

To find out more about her adventures with horses and the research she does to create Horse Diaries illustrations, visit her website, ruthsanderson.com.

Collect all the books in the Horse Diaries series!

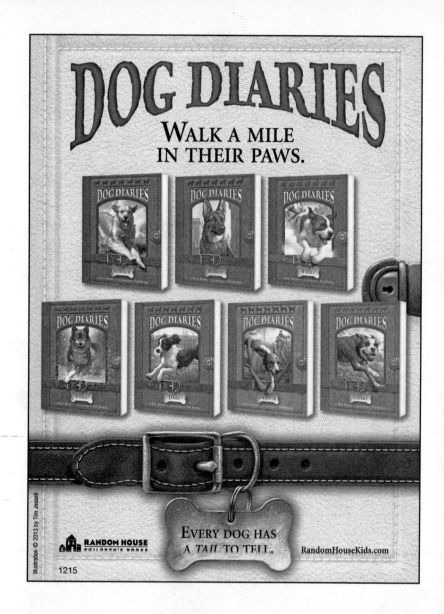